AF438923

Evincepub Publishing

Parijat Extension, Bilaspur, Chhattisgarh 495001
First Published by Evincepub Publishing 2021

Copyright © Deepa Singh 2021
All Rights Reserved.

ISBN: 978-93-5446-142-2

This book has been published with all reasonable efforts taken to make the material error-free after the consent of the author. No part of this book shall be used, reproduced in any manner whatsoever without written permission from the author, except in the case of brief quotations embodied in critical articles and reviews. The Author of this book is solely responsible and liable for its content including but not limited to the views, representations, descriptions, statements, information, opinions and references ["Content"]. The Content of this book shall not constitute or be construed or deemed to reflect the opinion or expression of the Publisher or Editor. Neither the Publisher nor Editor endorse or approve the Content of this book or guarantee the reliability, accuracy or completeness of the Content published herein and do not make any representations or warranties of any kind, express or implied, including but not limited to the implied warranties of merchantability, fitness for a particular purpose. The Publisher and Editor shall not be liable whatsoever for any errors, omissions, whether such errors or omissions result from negligence, accident, or any other cause or claims for loss or damages of any kind, including without limitation, indirect or consequential loss or damage arising out of use, inability to use, or about the reliability, accuracy or sufficiency of the information contained in this book.

Prisoner of dreams

Deepa Singh

EPILOGUE

(May ended the upcoming war with her power but in return she loses her keys and ability to use her power ever again)

It's the Consequences of overusing her power but in the end, she saved the day.

ABOUT THE BOOK

Is it wrong to dream? If yes, then why I must pay the price that I never expected to be, life is hell but dreams are jail

ABOUT THE AUTHOR

I hope you enjoyed my little story so I have a question for you.

What's your opinion on dream now?

Do they scare you or are they beautiful which turn into nightmare?

What is the first thing come in your mind when I say 'Dreams'.

Closed your eyes for a second and think of whatever comes in your mind when I say 'Dreams'.

"Is it good or bad dreams, scary or beautiful, lovely or nightmare."

"Do you remember the last night what you dreamed off"?

I don't remember my dreams most of time too when I wake up. But ...

If it is scary dreams I do remember every part of that dreams and kept having the nightmare and goosebumps every time I think of it.

Some of the dreams are so beautiful that I want then to be real. And some of them are so cheesy and embrassing that it Will make me smile or sometime make me sad.

Now, that's more than enough introduction for dream. (hehehe). Now shall I begin the story of 'Her' dream. For 'Her' her dreams become most lovely yet scary reality of her life.

State

As she wake up in a room with two man staring at her like they were waiting for her to

wake up... (In the old room with no furniture except the bed she is lying.)

She moves her hand and try to drag her body to sit supporting her back with pillow behind her back.

she felt headache. It was so painful as if she hit her head with wall.

She try to figure out what's going on here, trying to get the atmosphere but she couldn't remember anything what happened to her and how she gets here. How she get wounded in the first place. (That's the question she's thinking).

She looks up at one of the man making an eye contact with them. one of the man hands her a piece of note and then, both of them leave the room without saying anything, (leaving the door open.)

I, then unfold the piece of paper and saw there were bunch of routine to follow by specific task that need to be done on time.

I still don't know what's with all this mess. I try to get up and went near the window.

I was shocked to see that there were so many people working whether they are children, women, old man. people of all age Group were working under guard instructions.

I noticed all of them were wearing some kind of patterned bracelet on there hand.
 looking at my wrist, having the same kind of bracelet with red stone embedded on it.

21,21 someone came in the room shouting 21, NO.-21. (it was a one of the guard which I saw outside).

Looking at him. Guard - you, come.

Me. Where?

Guard- No.21 you have task assigned that you had to complete today on time.
He show me the changing room and give me an Number. It was no-21 identify card.

(in changing room)'I am slave here'. What the hell is going on. If only I could ask ....

There were many guards watching, instructing people regarding there work.

I changed into work cloth and came Outside.

The guard was still standing and waiting for me.
He made an eye contact with me and looked me from top to bottom.

What are you doing standing there? Come follow me and don't make me repeat again. - guard.

(Walking for almost 15 mins). We reached in a room full of books.

Arrange all that stuff and then follow your task given to you - 'guard Said'

All the work has to be done at the end of evening (voice came from behind).

Turning to see who's voice was. A wide chest with board shoulder, long beard man standing in front of me. Micheal (my name) - He said.

Guard you can go now. I will keep an eye on her. - (Micheal to guard)

"He seemed kind and understanding, I should ask him what I am doing here and ask more about this place" (in my head thinking).

You seemed to have lots of question. Am I right? - micheal.
Yes - (I answered).

Save it for later. After you finished your task for today - "Micheal said".

(What's with his attitude.) (In my mind).

In the evening (on the same day).

Finally Done.with all the work. - (No.21).

Meanwhile ...

Everyone coming after their work and some of them going to their next shift.

(Knock on the door)

 Everyone Gathered in the hall for dinner - "Guard".

(Hearing the announcement)- everyone rushed to dinner hall.

AT THE DINNER HALL

Big table and smell of delicious food.

"All of this making me hungry after all the work".

Man in old but extravagant dress Stand up, raised his hand for toast.

"Everyone take your seat and enjoy your meal".

taking the chair in corner table.

(Looking at my side)

Excuse me, mam (In humble voice, I asked one of the lady beside me).

"What is this place? Why are we working here and who are these men?" (I asked).

It seems you are newbie that everyone is talking about. Are you the no-21? " She replied ".

What do you mean? (Looking around, I noticed that Everyone was looking at me.)

Do you know who I am? And how I ended up here? - " I asked ".

Shhh! Lower your voice.

if they hear you not only but we will be punished too.

If you are so curious to know about your self. I suggest you to meet Harry.

 He seems to know you better. he's the one who bought you here in the first place.

-lady answered.

Where I can meet him - (I asked).

In the midnight you will she, shining giant sign of bull horn. You will see gate there.

That's the place where they keep all the prisoners who come from war. But be careful.

(In the midnight).

[Sneaking from my room and secretly walking through the hallway. I saw shining giant bull horn. Strange it was not even there in daytime.]

Somehow managed to get near the gate. Distracting guards is not easy. (But not going to give up.)

(Meanwhile).

I heard voice coming from the bush. I turn around to look and.....

May........ May....... May......

As I followed the voice. I saw a man with long beard waving at me. I went there, (hesitating)

You came after all- He said.
" The lady told me to help you get inside the prison ".
- (He).

You are may. Right? - He said.

Me? Did you say my name is May? - (I asked)

He nodded.

"Then, will you please help me to get through the gate so I can meet Harry.

Sure, but we have to hurry as we have not enough time .... (He said.)

come with me. -(He).

{He helped me like he said, and finally I'm able to know the truth about myself}.

[Reached to a dark room where he was there].

Harry?

May? Is that you? - (Harry said).

It's good to see you are doing good. -(harry).

I'm here to know about myself. As I don't have to much

time so please keep it simple and brief. - (I asked)

Okay. So where should I start from?

You see, I let myself caught intentionally so that I can meet you.

I came here to get you out of this place. -(Harry)

 You are my best friend and I will do anything to keep you safe.

Listen, I will tell you everything but first you have to get me out of this place. okay? - (Harry)

What? Wait a minute. How could I trust you that after you are free, you will help me. - (I asked)

you have no choice but to trust me May. I can guarantee you that I'm trustworthy.
Believe me. -(Harry)

Tip -Top tip-top- (shoes Voices)

"Guards are coming we should head back" - (The man with May).

 Is this joke? What I came for and what I get into myself- (May)

Do you want me to believe in your made-up story - "May said to Harry?

Who's there- (guard.)

Hurry May let's go - (Man pulling May arms).

Who was here Harry - (guard asked Harry)
Fairy girl-(Harry jokingly answered).
You and your stupid jokes - (guard).

we sneaked from there and returned to our sleeping room. With all those stupid efforts for what. How can I help him - (May talking to the Man)?

How I supposed to believe it? What to do? (May)
We can get help from her. - (Man).

Who? - (May)

"The lady" - (Man)

By the way, I didn't introduce myself earlier.

Myself sahil - (The man)

Sahil, Thanks for your help, toady. - (May)

You don't remember but I'm your closest friend - (Sahil in low voice, talking to himself)

What did you say-(May)

Nothing. good night. Rest, I will meet you soon er - (sahil leave the room).
.
.
.

I layed on my bed, thinking about this whole situation all night and end up fall asleep.

After all that efforts of finding truth about myself two days went like nothing.

And the things about to happen was unexpected.

TOW DAYS LATER.

ANNOUCEMEMT.

It is in order of superior; we hereby announce that the prisoners from giant bull horn will be Sentence to Death the day after tomorrow.

Everyone should gather at the execution site at 5 am in the morning.

What? Giant bull horn prisoners. (Everyone gossiping to each other).

It means the person I met on that day is going to die. (May).
What should I do? I have to save him.

He's the one who know me and where I came from? -
(may).

First, I need a plan.

Second, someone trust worthy who willing to help me.
- (may).

But who? Wait....I forgot about" the lady"

BELL RING.

Lunch time. Everyone leaving the work and gathering
in the dining room.

I sit on my usual spot and looking for her - (the lady
who introduced me to harry on that day.)

Finish eating as I was walking to put my plate in the
container I saw in front of my line, then I secretly put
a piece of note in her left pocket.

Later in the evening.

waiting at the place which I mentioned in the note.

"The lady" comes.

What you want this time? - (lady)

I need your help to save Harry. He's the one who can
tell me more about myself - (May)
Will you help me? - (May)

Seeta (my name), call me 'Seeta'.

Sure, but you are not the only one who want to help harry and other prisoner to escape to death penalty - ("Seeta").

What's the plan then- (May)

I will tell you everything on the day of execution. – "Seeta".

It seems there are many people who don't fully trust you - " Seeta"

Why? - (May)

Meet me on the same spot on that day in the midnight - "seeta"

EXECUTION DAY

Midnight (1:00 am)

It's been an hour. Where is she? -(May)

I felt an hand on my left shoulder as I get little freaked out -(May.)

Let's go and don't make any noise.
Put this on your shoes as it hides the shoe print on ground-" Seeta"

I followed her and we reached to an underground

tunnel which was hidden under the giant hollow tree. we then entered inside the tree. Surprisingly there was a hidden door which led us to the place where all the prisoner were held captive.

All the guard were making preparation for the execution ceremony.

we can clearly hear the sound of guard commotion under Tunnel as we were just beneath them.

{As we were walking, seeta Stopped and i almost bumped into her. I asked why do you stop. she said wait and then.}

Click-click, click-click (sound of door opening)

Door opened from the up about and an rope fell down.

Girl voice came from above.

Come - All clear.
Seeta, at first she Looked at me.and said

Wait here. I will be right back in 20 mins - Seeta
I nodded - (May)

AFTER SHE LEFT.

It was pitched dark that I can sense my body and could hear the sound of heart beat racing fast - May

20 mins later.

Sudden flash of light came to my face. I closed my eyes as it was so freaking bright.
Move, move (I heard seeta voice)

And other people voices coming from up about.

Everyone arrived safely (a familiar voice)
Harry – (May shocking reaction to see him in front of me)

Wow, you are looking pretty with the surprise look on your face--- (Harry)

Let's chat in the way - Harry.

Following the tunnel path. We all including, all the runway prisoners who escaped from prison were there.

{after walking for 30 mins we reached the end of tunnel.}

We looked up at the top of tunnel, there was rusty door with no look on to it. Harry move forward and with the help of five people he was able to open the door.

One by one everyone walking and making there way out of tunnel.

As we were out of the tunnel.

everyone was making shocking face as they saw huge wall in front of them.

{We heard the commotion of guards coming towards us.}

It's looks like stupid lazy guard realised that we escaped – Harry.

we are in the middle of getting caught and you are making stupid joke again-(Seeta)

Okay, okay. Everyone, this is it we have this wall and after that our freedom. - Harry.

How are we gonna climb that huge wall –

(one of us)

Chill guys. I got you- Harry.
[I saw a man at the top of wall throwing a rope from the top. It was none another than but Sahil]

Look, a rope - (May)

Capture Them - Guards were coming towards us with gun in there hand.

Everyone starts painking.

We will die. Hurry climbs the rope. (Prisoner)

one of Guards found out that we were in our way to escape. As they were coming towards us, more and more people climbing the wall.

Harry grabbed my hand and pulled me closer to him

Let's go or are you planning to get captured again --- Harry.

Again? What? wait ... (May)

Guards started firing guns, some of them die on the spot, and some of us managed to reached the top of wall.

Wait, there nothing in this side of wall. - (sudden realisation after reaching the top of wall).

Literally nothing. Looking back at Harry. - (May).

Believe me Just Jump with me - Harry.

I hesitatd first, then Harry grabbed me and we then jump of the wall with others...

{Secret room under basement of some place}

yo, you are finally awake.huh! - Harry.

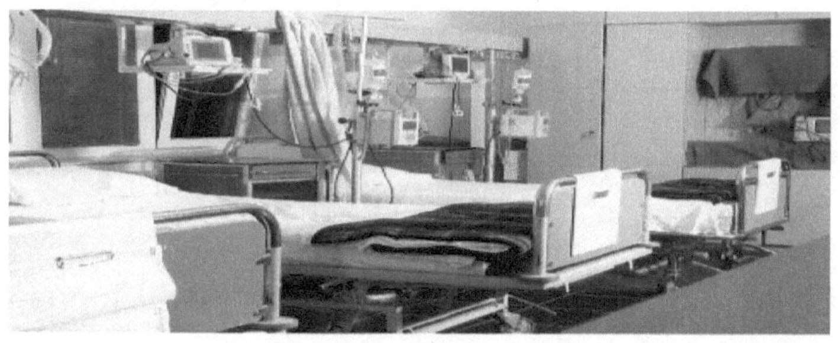

[opening my eyes in hospital ⊕.

I turned my head left seeing harry and others were lying in bed with me.]

 I can't believe the first thing I saw when I wake up is you - (May to Harry)

Nice one. - (Harry to May)

Did you sleep well?

i hope you are not gonna start questioning here in the hospital. (Harry)
Looks like you made it. May - (Man. 1)
She is truly one of special kind - (Man.2)

Yeah! Well let them chat with her as we are just gonna leave the room, (man 1, man 2)

We made it. How are you feeling – Harry

All over body pain other than that I'm as good as you. – (May to Harry)

Haha - Harry.

Look like you are in good shape though. - Harry.

How did we ended up here? I thought we die jumping from the wall - May.

Looks like I had to tell you everything from start. Because I can't run away with all your questions while I'm in bed -(Harry)

But since we stuck in here for a while let's catch-up. – Harry.

(Harry explaining everything)

Let's start from the beginning. you see,

In this world there are two types of people. One who are normal and others who born with special powers.

We are one of them, it's natural for normal human to feel insecure from our special power. It's human we are talking about who can do whatever to survive. when they find out that we are overpowering the population.

They started making there moves between normal human and special human.

As the time passes, these human started an organization which attack people like us who naturally born with the power. killing new born child to secretly kidnapping them to use run an experiment on them.

These organizations called (SPECIAL-A) They took human like us and befriend us and betrayed us.

Everything was going well until one day you decided to go undercover in there organization.

You said they are not bad people it just they are just afraid of our power. But if we convince them that we are not harmful to humanity they will definitely understand.

But our superior didn't listened to you. so, one day, you with your groups of friends escaped from the facility and went to the other side of human world.

When we heard the news about you.
We were shocked because you were our friend and we don't want you to get yourself killed by those people.

Week passed, Then month we heard no news from you and your friends with whom you went with.
That's where we were send as a volunteer to find you. When we reached to the other side of wall. We started searching for you disguised as human not using our power .

And thankfully, we found you but you were held as a experiment by those human. Not only they let you live as there object but killed every single one of your friends.

They were planning to use your special power against us.
As you have the Power which is very unique and different from us.

They kept you in a capsule where you were unconscious for months.

In mean time, I met seeta she was human but she was given power as an experiment.

She was truly kind and helpful in that situation to us. Because she felt the same thing as you did. she wanted peace between two races.

She dreams of some world where special and normal human can live in peace together.

You see, we Hide ourselves as one of there staff and find you there. To get you out of your unconscious mind to reality. We used seeta power to enter inside your mind and helped you get back to reality.

Everything you did and done so far was in your dreams.

From where you were in room to where we jumped off the wall All of them happened in your dream.

And, now here you are with us again.

After listening to Harry story.

I was shocked and surprise that how can everything feels so real but was not real at all - (May)

but how come I don't remember anything after walking up? - (May)

They erased your memories, so that when you are ready. They can have used you as your special weapon - (Seeta)

What happened after that? After we escaped?

Are we still inside the wall? - (May)

Yes, we are still inside the wall.

But safe, after your injuring completely heal. we will be resting and hiding here and then leave this place and can return home - (Harry)

Now you know the rest of thing.

I hope you will stop asking us what, how where all these 'w' question (Teasing in funny way) - Harry

What a mess I'm right now. - (May)

I feel empty inside even though I'm glad that you guys went through so much trouble but still not remembering anything it's scary - (May)

Don't worry time will heal everything and who knows, maybe you will remember everything anytime soon.

who knows? - (Seeta)

(cheering for May) yeah cheer up girl.

{WHILE IN FACILITY}.

One month later {In Base room of commander Tua)}

Sir, what Now? - solider 1

Shall we proceed with plan? - solider.2

No. wait till my order -(commander 'Tua to solider .1)

But sir, if we don't act now. It will be to late for us - solider 2

We have to wait till I get any news on Harry and their friends - commander Tua.

Sir, we got a good news from division – I, area - A that Harry and there friends, escaped from "Human sector wall-PHASEI". - solider -3 (entering inside the room)

Good. Thank for the news. Now, get your men to help them. - (commander Tua. to solider-2).
After Harry, May and others return.

Welcome Back Harry, May, Seeta all of you welcome home - (General Rem greeting all the survivors).

Nice to be back home - survivor. '1'

Yeah, now we can rest all we want - Survivor '2'

I want to eat something first - Survivor '2'

(on the same day, In resting room)

Everything celebrating there friends return from enemy base.

Tring...... Ringggg........ (Red alarm)

What's happening - commander Tua to solider besides him.

Sir, enemy attack. They found out about escapee and that the everyone from there laboratory escaped. They came near our base with there solider to attack us. - (Solider 1 to commander tua).
Gather everyone from special task force and get them ready to counter attack - commander Tua.

Yes, sir - Solider -1(ring the alarm for emergency attack)

I knew this day would come. Eventually.

Human, special one can never be together.
- (commander tua).

What would happened if both of us fight to survivor - (solider-2 asking to commander tua).

[While on the other side, where Harry and there friends were resting came to know that they are underattack]

Enemy continued to attack us. Many of our solider while others were trying to counterattack. But because of the enemy advance techgun infuse with power were strong enough to kill anyone with power.

{Who would be responsible for this - [one of the survivor came to the room and start blaming May for all of this mess}.

May, if only you wouldn't went to enemy base for so called peace. We would be living in harmony - (others man in the room agreeing to the person talking to May).

[Everyone starts blaming May. May who still don't remember anything about her past feels little hurt and leave the room by running away. Where Harry was trying to handle the people in the room].

May ran away from room and start running to place where she can be alone.

What I'm supposed to do? I don't even remember my past. Yet all these people are blaming me - (may in crying voice).

What if it's because of me. Is it wrong to hope that all of us leave together as one?

A place where everyone can be live equally, Peacefully.

Is it wrong to dream of such world - (May)

I don't even know how to use my power if only I could help to stop this attack.

" You can do only if want to"
Who.... Whose here?
 Come forward –(May looking around).

" just look in over here"

C..... Commander Tua. - May (in startled voice).
Yes - (commander tua).

Look, I'm not critizing you for what have you done so far.

But as you know every action has its own reaction.

Your actions bring danger to our lives, not only to your friends but to our people, our families too. - Commander Tua.

How could I do such thing? I wish it was turn into dream? - May

Come with me- "Commander Tua"

(Commander Tua take May to secret room where she can see giant capsule).

You don't know how to use your power but don't worry. I have a plan after what you just said while ago - (commander tua to May).

This machine is made for that purpose. IT can analyse the person inner power and use it as it's maximum. - Commander Tua
Really? I mean.
Why are you showing me this as if I could use my power to turn reality into dream -(May).
You can - (commander tua looking at May).

You, only you possess special power called 'DREAL' which can turn dream to reality and reality into dream.)
.

That's the very reason enemy wants to control you and your Power. - (commander tua).

How can you be so sure that I'm the one who can do it - May.

shall we try -(Tua)

I....... Okay...... (May)

So, let get this thing started, shall we? – (commander Tua).

But.

Before that I want to warn you that we haven't yet use this machine before on anyone so it's just that anything could happen to you.

I'm not sure, but maybe death in worst case - Commander Tua.

If I'm the one who can stop this enemy attack and an upcoming danger with my power. I will do it with my life on to it – May
[Commander Tua noticed that may was shacking with fear, her voice was filled with fear but her brave act made him proud]

Get inside I will start the machine. - (commander Tua
to May).
And....... This machine only can maximize your power.
So you just have to focus on   that thing that you
wanted to change the most.

Am I clear? - Commander Tua

[May nodded her head inside the capsule).
.

.

in an blink of eye everything changed.

[War ended both side agreed on agreement that none
of the them will ever interfere in in each other
business].

Two Months Later (In facility training room).

[Seeta asked May when she entered in tne training
room.]

How are you? Good? – Seeta

Hmmm feeling much better – May

How did you do that? I mean to say that it's still
mystery that on that day. Enemy re turned to there
base as if nothing happened.
And after the very next day both the side signed the
pact that none of them will ever interfere in each other
matter - Harry.

hmm. should I tell you or not.

Let's keep its a secret - May.

I will tell you some other time. It's kind of boring to tell you when I'm on the wheelchair - May

[Everyone lauging].

****

On the other side of room.

Commander Tua talking to an person.

[Did you see? I told you she's the one who will be perfect for this. So I shall consider this as a deal.]

Person - it's just a beginning not end.

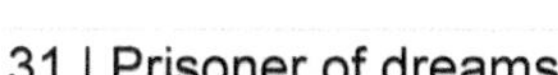

www.ingramcontent.com/pod-product-compliance
Lightning Source LLC
La Vergne TN
LVHW051515170726
843492LV00002B/943